The Beaver's Tail

adapted from a Shoshone folktale

Carrie Weston
Illustrated by Cecilia Johansson

RIGBY

Long, long ago there was a beautiful river.

It

  ran

    down

      a

        steep

          hill.

The water was deep and clean and
sparkled in the sun.

The river was the home of two friends –
Hanee, the beaver and Tindui, the otter. Hanee
lived on one side of the river and Tindui lived
on the other.

3

Hanee, the beaver, liked to work hard. All day long she chewed down trees, and carried logs to make her home bigger and stronger.

Tindui, the otter, liked to play. All day long he splashed about in the water, and chased his tail. Every day, Tindui watched the busy beaver working hard. "I wish Hanee would stop working just for a while and play with me," he thought.

Then, one day, Tindui had a clever idea. He began to build something.

After a while, he called across the river to his friend, "Hanee! Look at what I have built. It's a slide!"

Hanee didn't answer.

"I bet you can't build a slide as big as this one," said Tindui.

Hanee stopped working and looked up.

Tindui smiled to himself. His plan was working.

"I bet I can," Hanee called across the river.
"I can build a bigger and better slide than you
have ever seen!"

The beaver quickly began moving all the rocks
and logs she could find.

All morning Hanee worked. She worked harder
than Tindui had ever seen.

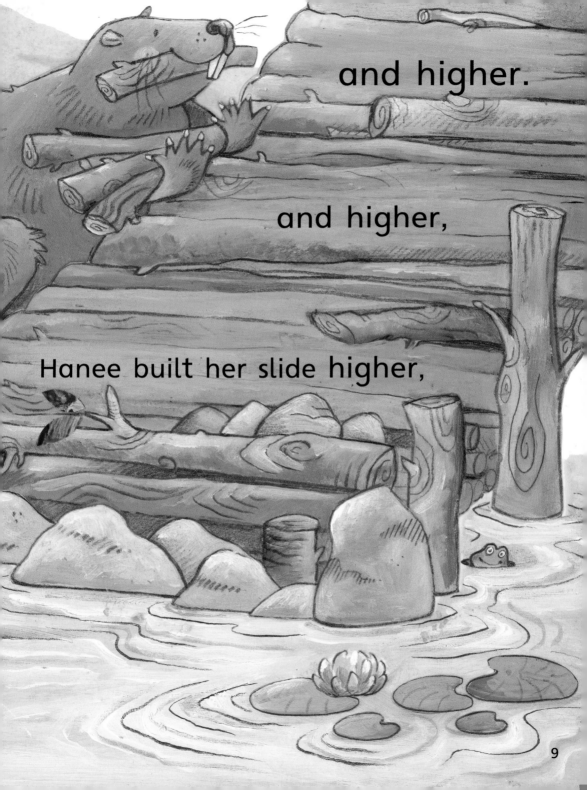

and higher.

and higher,

Hanee built her slide higher,

When Hanee had finished, she called to the otter, "Look at my slide! I bet this is the biggest and best slide you have ever seen."

Then she climbed to the top of her slide and slid down.

bump!

bump!

bump!

"Ouch!" cried Hanee. "Those logs are hard. Next time, I will have to sit on my tail."

Hanee climbed up to the top of her slide again. This time, she sat on her tail and slid all the way down in to the sparkling water. Tindui climbed up the slide and slid down after her.

They climbed and slid and splashed all afternoon. They had great fun, and for once, Hanee forgot all about work.

"Hanee!" laughed Tindui. "Your slide is the biggest and the best that I have ever seen. But just look at your tail!"

Hanee turned to look. Her beautiful tail was now as flat as a paddle, and there wasn't a hair left on it!

"Oh, Tindui!" cried the beaver. "Look what this foolish playing has done to my tail!"

Hanee ran back to her home. She was ashamed. She had played all day and not done any work. And now just look at her tail.

But soon Hanee found that her new tail was very useful.

She could swim faster, and twist and turn more quickly under the water.

When there was danger, Hanee could splash the water with her tail and warn her friends.

And she could work harder.

Hanee began to like her new tail very much.

To this day, all beavers have tails like Hanee.
They are very flat and very scaly and
very, **very** useful.